Welcome to Your World

SMRITI HALLS illustrated by JAIME KIM

WALKER BOOKS
AND SUBSIDIARIES
LONDON • BOSTON • SYDNEY • AUCKLAND

Welcome, little baby,
round your mama curled.
Welcome, little baby.
Welcome to your world.

Look up to the sky. Can you see the sun?
Feel its kiss upon your cheek. Morning has begun.

Look out to the forests.
Look out to the trees.
Can you see the butterflies?
Can you see the bees?

Look into the ocean, with its waves of blue.

Can you see the turtles and all the fishes, too?

Look up to the mountains, reaching for the sky.
Listen for the eagles, soaring, swooping by.

Look out to the ice caps, with their peaks of white.

Do you see the polar bears in the Arctic light?

Can you feel the raindrops landing on your nose?
Can you feel the waterfall tickling your toes?

Taste the juicy berries. Smell the blossoms sweet.

Hear the gentle whisper
of the waving fields of wheat.

Listen to the creatures of the air and land and sea,
living whole and happily, living wild and free.

Now look up to the stars, twinkling out in space.
Look up to the moon, lighting up your face.

Welcome to your world – it loves you through and through.

Welcome to your world …

will you love it, too?

For Eleanor Yolande and her marvellous mama, Lizzie;
welcome to your world
S. H.

For Riu
J. K.

First published 2020 by Walker Books Ltd
87 Vauxhall Walk, London SE11 5HJ

This edition published 2021

2 4 6 8 10 9 7 5 3 1

Text © 2020 Smriti Prasadam-Halls

Illustrations © 2020 Jaime Kim

This book has been typeset in Columbus

Printed in China

British Library Cataloguing in Publication Data:
a catalogue record for this book is available from the British Library

ISBN 978-1-4063-9428-3

www.walker.co.uk